Little LOLA'S

GREAT BIG LIFE

Story & Illustrations by
LUCIE RICE

Lola, the little brown dog,
is lonely and bored.

She can't go very far, and there is not much to do within the walls of her tall, wooden fence. She spends her days barking at squirrels, hunting for bugs, and digging for treasure.

Lola is **VERY** good at digging.

But this is not enough. Little Lola is tired of being lonely and longs for a life full of **great big** adventure.

One day, Lola notices a beam of light shining through a small hole in the fence.

When she peeks through the hole, she **thinks** she sees a bright and happy place beyond.

She can even imagine herself on the other side of the fence, living a life full of **great big** adventure.

She sees herself going on fast rides

and enjoying fantastic views.

She sees herself sailing the high seas

and having high-flying fun.

And she sees herself meeting exotic animals and traveling to faraway lands.

But when she looks away, she is reminded that she is still stuck on the wrong side of the fence. And this makes Lola very sad.

So sad that she doesn't feel like barking at squirrels, hunting for bugs, or digging for treasure.

But, wait. She is **VERY** good at digging, so...

She digs.

And tugs.

And then digs some more.

At last, she is **FREE!**
Lola has dug her way through
to the other side of the fence.

But things are not quite as bright and happy as she hoped they would be.

She can't seem to
find the fast rides and
fantastic views.

Those high seas and all that
high-flying fun are hard to spot, too.

And the animals she sees are not very exotic and the lands are not nearly far enough away.

Lola, the little brown dog, is tired.
She goes looking for a place to rest
and sees a bright spot ahead.

As she gets closer, Lola sees a little door that is just her size and decides to peek inside.

This time, life on the other side
is just as bright and happy as she hoped it would be.

And this is when Lola's **great big** adventure truly begins.

These days, Lola, the little brown dog, is no longer lonely and bored. She spends her time going on fast rides and seeing fantastic views. She sails the high seas and has high-flying fun. And she meets exotic animals and travels to faraway lands.

But best of all, little Lola has found something
else she is **VERY** good at: Living a life full of **great big love.**

"Two Headed Monster"

ABOUT

Lucie Rice is a Nashville based illustrator and designer who began her creative endeavors at a very early age, drawing portraits and writing stories about the beloved family dog. Many moons (and college loans) later, she is still at it. Always inspired by her love for animals, she spends her days creating quirky characters and creatures, and loving on her own furry brood: Lola, the real-life little brown dog, and big Hank, Lola's boxer brother. Both dogs were rescues, and it was through these experiences that Lucie became educated and active in the animal welfare cause. She regularly donates her time and talents to animal rescue organizations on both a local and national level. See more of her work (and meet plenty more furry friends and characters) at **www.lucierice.com.**

LOLA
(in real-life)

Meet little Lola, handsome Hank, and lucky Lucie

PHOTO CREDIT: HARMONY DESIGNS PHOTOGRAPHY

CPSIA information can be obtained
at www.ICGtesting.com
Printed in the USA
LVIC06n1924071115
461362LV00004B/7